# GHOSTS

A

## Strange Science

B O O K

Sylvia Funston

*Illustrations by* Joe Weissmann

Owl Books are published by Greey de Pencier Books Inc.
51 Front Street East, Suite 200, Toronto, Ontario M5E 1B3

The Owl colophon is a trademark of Owl Children's Trust Inc.
Greey de Pencier Books Inc. is a licensed user of trademarks of Owl Children's Trust Inc.

Distributed in the United States by Firefly Books (U.S.) Inc.
230 Fifth Avenue, Suite 1607, New York, NY 10001

We acknowledge the financial support of the Canada Council for the Arts, the Ontario
Arts Council, and the Government of Canada through the Book Publishing Industry
Development Program (BPIDP) for our publishing activities.

**Dedication**
To Nick, with love and gratitude

**Cataloguing in Publication Data**
Funston, Sylvia
      Ghosts

"A strange science book".
Includes index.
ISBN 1-894379-19-5 (bound)       ISBN 1-894379-20-9 (pbk.)

1. Ghosts — Juvenile literature.  I. Weissmann, Joe, 1947–    .    II. Title.

BF1461.F86    2001       j133.1       C2001-930426-9

Design & art direction: Word & Image Design Studio Inc.
Illustrations: Joe Weissmann
Editor: Kat Mototsune

**Photo Credits**
Pages 6, 37: Fortean Picture Library; 11: Gianni Dagli Orti/CORBIS/MAGMA; 12: Kim
Taylor/Bruce Coleman, Inc.; 14: J.C. Carton/Bruce Coleman, Inc.; 15: J. Sarapochiello/
Bruce Coleman, Inc.; 18–19: Rex A. Butcher/Bruce Coleman, Inc.; 21, 27, 30 (main):
Bettmann/CORBIS/MAGMA; 22: Ernest A. Janes/Bruce Coleman, Inc.; 23 (optical illusions
artwork): Dianne Eastman; 28: Oscar Burriel/Science Photo Library; 30 (inset): Hulton-
Deutsch Collection/CORBIS/MAGMA; 31: Andrew Brown/Ecoscene/CORBIS/MAGMA;
32: Images Colour Library; 38: Telegraph Group Ltd./Eddie Mulholland 2001; 39: Janet &
Colin Bord/Fortean Picture Library

Printed in Hong Kong

A      B      C      D      E      F

# Contents

# It's SPOOOOKY!

**Y**ou wake in the middle of the night, hungry for a peanut butter sandwich. Deciding it's probably best not to switch on the light, you slowly grope your way to the kitchen. Suddenly, a white shape looms out of the dark. Does the little voice inside your head tell you there must be a perfectly normal explanation for the shape? No; it shrieks, "Ghost!" and your knees turn to jelly.

Around the world, millions of people claim to have come in contact with ghosts, the spirits of dead people. But every major religion is based on the belief in some kind of life after death, so that's not too surprising. This book isn't going to question religious beliefs. But, like the ghosthunters who investigate hauntings, it is going to look at several kinds of ghosts and see if there might be more than one explanation for them.

Contrary to what books or movies show, not all ghosts float around under a white sheet, moaning and dragging clanking chains behind them. They appear in many different forms (not all human) and for different reasons. We know this because ghosthunters have gathered lots of information about ghosts. But remember that science doesn't have the answer to everything. Even if ghosthunters can find natural explanations for up to 98 percent of ghostly events, that still leaves 2 percent a mystery—and a very spooky one at that!

# Spooky
# QUESTIONS

While taking photographs for *Country Life* magazine in 1936, Captain Provand shot this picture at Raynham Hall in England at four o'clock in the afternoon. His assistant saw the figure and cued the Captain to shoot. The photographer was surprised to find that he had captured an image of the Brown Lady—especially because the famous ghost was known to haunt the Hall at midnight! Many experts think this photograph is authentic. What do you think?

# Have You Seen a Ghost?

If you live in North America or northern Europe, you stand an almost 50 percent chance of believing that ghosts exist. And millions of people around the world claim they've actually met—if not seen—a ghost. Surprisingly few ghosts are visible. Of those that are, some might look solid enough to touch, but others are indistinct, like an old photograph that's fading from view.

Many ghostly encounters involve mysterious footsteps, whisperings, rapping or rustling sounds. Sometimes you can detect ghosts by sudden, powerful smells: if you're lucky, the delicate perfume of flowers or the sweet aroma of burning wood; if not, the stench of rotting flesh. Other ghosts make their presence known through sudden cold breezes, or by the touch of their cold, ghostly fingers. And some give a place a bad—or sometimes a good—feeling.

Have millions of people encountered ghosts? Or have they decided they have because they can't come up with a better explanation? Nobody has yet come up with definite proof that ghosts do or don't exist. As you'll find out, most (but maybe not all) ghostly encounters can be explained by perfectly everyday events.

**I believe in ghosts!**

## Do a Boo Poll

**Do you have a lot of spooked-out friends? Or do they think the only thing that goes bump in the night is their sister falling out of the top bunk? Survey your friends, family and classmates to find out how many of them believe in ghosts. Multiply the number of believers by 100, and divide by the number of people you polled to find the percentage of believers. Do your numbers vary from the 50 percent national average?**

## Sheep or Goat?

Have you ever thought of someone and suddenly the phone rings and they're on the line? Some people call that a sixth sense, when you know something intuitively, without using your five known senses (other people call it a coincidence). About 50 years ago, a psychologist did some experiments and discovered that people who believe that ESP (extrasensory perception) tests work do better in them than people who don't. She named believers "sheep" and nonbelievers "goats." What does this have to do with ghosts? Well, sheep people are more inclined to come up with a supernatural explanation for things they don't understand than goats are. Would you say "baa" or "boo" to a ghost?

# Spooky
# QUESTIONS

Ghosts didn't walk through walls in the 17th century. Reports from that time say they opened doors and shut them afterwards—sometimes they were polite enough to knock!

## Can Ghosts Exist?

**Warning: Don't answer the door if a ghost knocks.**

Ghosts have many strange habits, one of which is walking through solid walls. Don't they realize that two objects aren't supposed to occupy the same space at the same time? Does the fact that they do walk through walls mean that they must be figments of our imagination?

## Is Anyone Out There?

Space is far from empty. Any object passing through space disturbs tiny particles of matter, creating energy patterns that last long after it leaves. This modern view of space sounds eerily like the ancient idea that we're surrounded by an energy field called the "ether." That's where ghosts are supposed to live, and psychics are thought to be able to tap into the ether to see them. The rest of us have to be content with wondering what's out there.

Ghost believers might say, "If quarks can do it, why can't ghosts?" In case you're wondering, quarks aren't sounds made by ducks with sore throats. They're unimaginably small particles that vibrate at high speed at the heart of every atom in the universe. When scientists discovered them in the 1960s, they could hardly believe their eyes. Like ghosts, quarks pass straight through solid objects.

Scientists would argue that the amazing behavior of quirky quarks has nothing to do with ghosts and doesn't prove that it's possible for ghosts to exist. But, at the very least, the fact that quarks exist suggests that we should keep an open mind about things we don't fully understand.

## Life After Death?

People who have been revived by paramedics or doctors after their hearts stopped beating often report very similar experiences. They float out of their bodies, hear a loud buzzing noise and move through a tunnel towards a bright light, where dead loved ones are waiting to greet them. Eventually they wake to find themselves back in their own bodies. Many people who go through this "near death experience" feel they have proof of life after death. But scientists are more likely to think that what these people experience really happens inside their heads, when their brain's supply of oxygen runs critically low.

## How Ghosts Are Made

In many cultures there's a belief that we each have more than one body (and you thought one was enough to keep clean!). According to one such belief, when we die we pass from our physical body into an energy body, which is attached by a silver thread. The energy body acts as a bridge to our spiritual body. If all is well, we then pass into our spiritual body, the thread is broken and we are released to make the journey to the next life. If all is not well—if we have met a sudden, violent end or aren't given a proper burial—we remain trapped in our energy body and become a ghost.

**That's the spirit!**

The Inuit of North America's far north have a traditional belief that people have a "life soul" that brings life to the body and dies with it, and a "free soul" that lives on in another world after death. The free soul is the one that might return as a ghost. In China, there's a similar belief that each person has two spirits: the *Shin* or good spirit and the *Kuei* or bad spirit. If a corpse does not receive a proper burial, its *Kuei* is free to wander.

## Have a Good Journey

People all over the world perform special rituals over dead bodies to help the spirits of the dead move on, and prevent them from returning to haunt the living. For the ancient Egyptians the physical remains of the dead had to be preserved, since the spirit, or "ka," continued to live in the body. They crammed their tombs with food, treasure and personal belongings for use in the next life. They even put a book in the tomb, telling the dead how to reach their final destination. This picture below comes from one of these Books of the Dead.

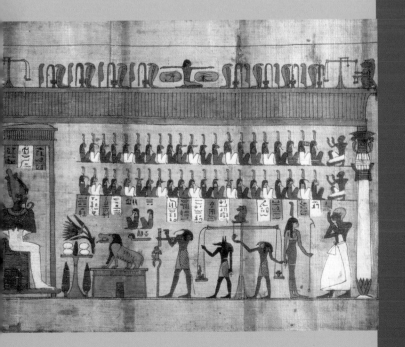

## Don't Come Back!

People go to great lengths to prevent a ghost from finding its way back home. In the Solomon Islands, a funeral procession never returns home by the same route it travels to the graveyard. In many societies, the bodies of the dead are securely bound to prevent them walking. Some Australian aboriginal people used to make absolutely certain the dead couldn't walk by breaking their legs. In Germany, it's the dead person's pottery that is broken; it's done at the nearest crossroads to confuse the phantoms, who have no map-reading skills.

# Spooky BELIEFS

In many cultures, there are superstitions connecting birds with death. The Tsimshian people of the Pacific Northwest have a belief that the souls of the recently dead turn into owls.

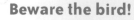

**Beware the bird!**

## Death Omens

Birds have long been seen as omens of death, especially black birds like ravens or night birds like owls. A wild bird that flies into a house is supposed to foretell a death in the family. But omens of death aren't limited to birds. In some parts of the world the wailing of a banshee—a female death spirit that attaches itself to a family—should be heeded. Better have a medical check-up if you start seeing ghost lights floating over the ground at night. And if word gets out that a phantom coach pulled by a phantom black horse and driven by a headless horseman has stopped by your house, it's time to order a coffin.

Of course, there are rational reasons for all these events (well, maybe not for the phantom coach). But scientists have discovered that if you come down with a serious illness shortly after an owl flies across your path, you're more likely to think the two events are connected than if it happened to someone else. In that case, you're more likely to think it was pure coincidence.

But why do people have so many superstitions about death to begin with? Spiritual beliefs help us come to terms with the idea of death, but superstitious beliefs help us think that we might have some control over it by foretelling when it will happen. Commonplace events take on a new, superstitious significance if they're followed almost immediately by someone's death.

## ARE YOU SUPERSTITIOUS?

**1**
What would you do if you spilled some salt?

**2**
What do you do when you come across a crack in the sidewalk?

**3**
Would you walk under or around a ladder?

You'll find explanations for your actions on page 40.

Now ask your friends and family these questions.

## Ghost Lights

If you ever see ghost lights in a cemetery, you can be certain of one thing: the whole place is waterlogged. Scientists have thought for years that these strange, dancing lights are linked to methane gas produced by bacteria in the waterlogged ground. But something has to ignite it. The answer: farmyard manure. It contains diphosphane gas, which burns spontaneously when it meets air. So if you do come across any ghost lights, watch where you step!

13

# BELIEFS

## The Spookiest Night of the Year

Every October 31, millions of kids dress up in scary costumes, bang on people's doors and yell, "Trick or treat!" It's a night full of fun and good things to munch. But do you know what Halloween is really all about?

People used to believe that Halloween was the best time of year to communicate with the dead. Its full name is All Hallows' Eve, the night before All Hallows' or All Souls' Day. It's the one

**Get out the ghostly treats!**

night in the year when the boundary between the living and the dead can be passed through, so the souls of the dead are free to roam among the living. The custom of trick-or-treating might have started when people went out begging for soul cakes to be offered to the dead.

In China, people perform special ceremonies for the souls of their dead ancestors throughout the year. For two weeks during autumn, at the time of the Seventh Moon, special ceremonies acknowledge ghosts who have no living descendants to take care of them. These ghosts are lonely and hungry, so food is prepared for them. And at dusk, the hungry ghosts are remembered on streams and rivers throughout the land by thousands of tiny boats bearing candles.

## Welcome Back

The Japanese people celebrate their equivalent of All Souls' Day in July. It's known as Obon, or the "Feast of the Lanterns." Special lanterns are hung at the gates of houses to guide the spirits of the dead back home, where they are entertained with food and gifts. There's even dancing!

## The Day of the Dead

In Mexico, the festival that remembers and celebrates the dead lasts three days. Gifts are made on Halloween for the *angelitos*, little children who have died (see above). According to belief, they come home around midnight, enjoy their gifts, then leave. The following day, living children enjoy the treats made for the *angelitos* while adults prepare a feast for the older spirits who will soon arrive to join in the festivities. On the last day of the festival, the Day of the Dead, neighbors share food and drink and tell stories about the dead, who gather around to listen. Finally, satisfied that they've been remembered for another year, the dead return to their graves.

## When is the best time to see a ghost?

That's simple—nighttime. Don't worry if you can't stay awake all night; dreamtime is a good time to tune into ghosts, especially the special kind of dream known as a "waking dream." In a waking dream you're fast asleep, but you dream that you've woken up. You can tell you're having a waking dream by the eerie glow in the background and the fact that familiar objects often seem to be lit from within. This strange lighting crops up in lots of ghost sightings. So if you find yourself face to face with a ghost, check out the lighting—if it's weird, quit worrying. Oh, and you'll never be attacked by a ghost in your bed—blankets and duvets are naturally ghostproof.

## Are graveyards the most haunted places?

Strangely enough, no. But if you think about it, it makes sense. Ghosts usually haunt the place where they died. How many people have you heard of who died in a graveyard? That doesn't mean that graveyards are totally phantom-free. Every graveyard supposedly has at least one ghost, the spirit of the first person to have been buried there. This ghostly guardian is there to keep out evil spirits and unwanted intruders. Maybe that's why people do all kinds of superstitious things—like whistling—when they pass a graveyard.

# Why do ghosts walk through walls?

Some ghosts are doomed to repeat the actions that ended in their death. They can't change their behavior or the route they followed when they were alive. It doesn't matter that the house has been completely renovated several times, and that staircases have been moved and walls knocked down or built somewhere else. Ghosts must follow the original floorplan of the house. If that means climbing a now non-existent staircase or walking through a wall, that's the way it has to be.

# Are there animal ghosts?

During the American Civil War, a Confederate spy was captured with his dog. He was sentenced to death and, unknown to him, his dog was taken away and killed. Next day, as the condemned man faced the firing squad, he saw his dog running toward him and called out to it. The firing squad didn't see a dog, but the colonel in charge did. It so terrified him that he couldn't give the order to fire. Finally he dismissed the firing squad. That night, Confederate soldiers succeeded in setting the condemned man free. Only then did he learn that his dog had returned from the dead to save his life.

# Ghosts Attached to
# PLACES

Stonehenge in England is the most famous site of sacred standing stones in the world. It might also be the world's biggest sound recorder!

## Phantom Battle

The Battle of Shilo in Tennessee, one of the bloodiest conflicts of the American Civil War, raged for two days in April 1862. By the time the smoke cleared, 24,000 men had lost their lives. Gradually, over the following months, strange reports started to trickle out of Tennessee. The sounds of battle—gunfire, the clash of sabers and bayonets and the terrible screams of dying men—could still be heard coming from the deserted battlefield.

## Instant Replay Ghosts

Have you ever suddenly had a bad feeling about a place? It's an old idea that tragic or violent events can somehow be recorded on the atmosphere of a place, and can later be detected by psychic people. It's thought they might hear or see things that others can't, as if they're witnessing replays of a past event. The ghosts in these replays are said to seem unaware of living observers. They always do the same thing, and they're only visible from one viewpoint. Over time the images become transparent. The sound might remain clear long after the images disappear, but it too eventually fades away.

Is it possible that some ghosts are energy recordings of past events? No one can explain atmospheric recordings, but researchers have discovered some interesting things about stone. For instance, certain types of stone, especially those at ancient sacred sites like Stonehenge, can have a powerful effect on some people. Researchers investigating these sites around the world have detected different types of energy coming from them, including magnetism, radioactivity and sound waves so high in frequency only bats could hear them. There is a theory that information can somehow be stored as electrical energy in highly crystalline stone, then released again when conditions are right. If there is someone standing nearby whose brain reacts to the release of this electrical energy, they might possibly hear or see things from the past.

## Ghost Camp

Constable Cecil Denny served with the Northwest Mounted Police in Alberta. One day in 1875, a thunderstorm forced him to seek shelter. The sound of drumming led him into the woods, where he came upon a clearing. It contained about 20 lodges and was bustling with activity. Denny thought it was unusual that the people were moving about rather than staying sheltered from the rain. Suddenly, a searing flash of lightning struck a nearby tree, and when he looked again the camp had disappeared. He was so terrified, he ran. The next day he returned and found evidence of an old Cree campsite, but the rival Blackfoot tribe had attacked and killed everyone there many years earlier.

## Hup, Two, Three, Four

If stone can record sound vibrations, then it makes sense that sounds repeated over and over again will be recorded most strongly. Maybe this explains why phantom Roman soldiers are said to still patrol Hadrian's Wall in northern England. The wall was built to keep out northern invaders, so over the years it would have echoed to the sounds of thousands of marching feet. So too would the Via Decumana, a Roman road that runs beneath the Treasurer's House in the English city of York. A group of 20 Roman soldiers and a cart-horse have been seen marching through the cellars of the house. But because the road would have been about 45 cm (18 inches) below the cellar floor, they appear to be walking *in* the floor, and are only seen from the knees up.

**All aboard the ghost ship!**

## Mechanical Ghosts

On January 26, 1923, a ship left Cape Town in South Africa for Britain. The night set in, overcast and very dark. At 15 minutes past midnight, four sailors sighted a strange light ahead. Eventually, they were able to make out a two-masted sailing vessel heading toward them. No navigation lights were visible, but the entire vessel glowed. The two officers, the helmsman and a cadet watched it approach until it was about 800 m (1/2 mile) away, and then it disappeared. Had they seen the legendary *Flying Dutchman*?

There are various accounts of how the *Flying Dutchman* became a ghost ship. In the Dutch version, the captain vowed to sail around the Cape of Storms, now known as the Cape of Good

Hope, despite the storm that was blowing. Nothing his terrified crew said would change his mind. The vessel was no match for the mountainous seas. All the souls on board were lost, doomed to forever haunt the treacherous waters off the Cape in their phantom ship.

If ghosts really are the spirits of the dead, how can a ship become a ghost? Maybe the *Flying Dutchman* is an instant replay ghost, recorded on the turbulent atmosphere of the storm-tossed Cape. Or maybe it's a mirage of an actual ship just out of sight over the horizon. In certain conditions, light bouncing off a ship below the horizon can be bent so that its image is cast up into the air, against the clouds. But how this could happen in complete darkness is a mystery.

## The Lost Griffon

*The Griffon*, built in Niagara, New York, in 1679, was the largest Great Lakes ship of its time. She made a successful maiden run to Washington Island, Wisconsin, in August of that year to take on a cargo of fur. A month later, *The Griffon* set out on the return run to Niagara. According to legend, the ship sailed through a crack in the ice and vanished. It's said that her ghost can still be seen drifting about Lake Huron on foggy nights.

## The Black Train

On April 27, 1865, a black-draped funeral train (see below) made a slow journey from Washington DC to Springfield, Illinois. It carried the body of the assassinated US president, Abraham Lincoln. The route was lined with distraught people who had come to pay their last respects to their leader. Lincoln's ghost has been seen in the White House by many people. But the phantom of his entire black funeral train is supposed to appear every April 27, always following the same route it took all those years ago!

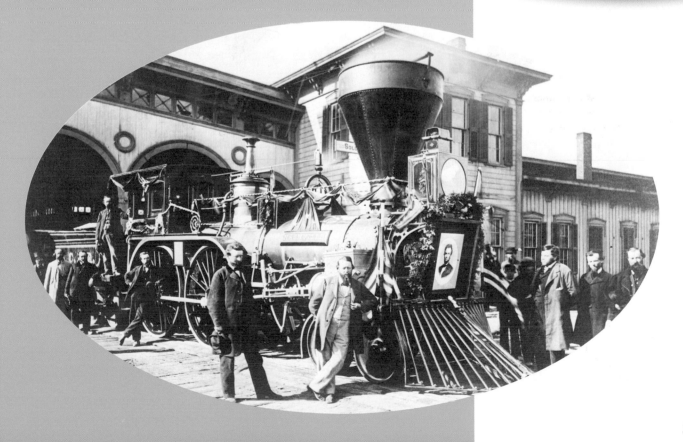

# Ghosts Attached to PLACES

The Tower of London is said to be one of the most haunted buildings in the world. This shouldn't come as a surprise if you think about all the people who died or were executed there over the centuries.

## Fungus Fear

Could some ghosts be the result of an allergic reaction to fungal spores? Many haunted buildings are very old. And old buildings have more than their share of molds and mildews. One idea is that fungal spores in old houses can upset our brain chemistry, unleashing feelings of sudden terror. Unable to account for this emotional upset, and already thinking the place is haunted, the visitor might well imagine the ghost they expect to see.

## Not You Again!

Like Lincoln's funeral train, some ghosts turn up in only one place and only on the anniversary of a traumatic event. It's almost as if they need a whole year to pull themselves together again for another appearance. The Tower of London is reportedly visited by a ghostly white shape on the anniversary of the execution of Lady Jane Grey. Poor Lady Jane. She was Queen of England for only ten days in 1553 before her husband, King Henry VIII, muttered, "Off with her head." People visit the Tower every February 12 expecting to see her ghost, and sometimes they say they do.

Ghosts with sad histories give off unhappy vibes. But another type of ghost usually gives off very cheery vibes. This ghost returns by choice to a place that made it very happy. The happy ghost that returns to its favorite haunts is known as a revenant, from the French word *revenir*, meaning "to return."

You can see how you might think a place is haunted if you suddenly feel sad or happy when you enter it. But what, besides the presence of a ghost, could possibly cause sudden mood swings? Some people are very sensitive to different types of energy fields. The kind of energy that's released during earth tremors, for instance, can scramble brainwaves, causing sensitive people to see things that aren't there and experience different emotions. Could some people's awareness of ghostly atmospheres and "presences" in haunted houses be caused by a kind of short circuit in their brains?

## DON'T BELIEVE YOUR EYES

Your brain filters all the information it receives from your senses and fills in any blanks to make the world appear the way you expect it to be. So if you believe in ghosts, you're more likely to see them. Look at the images below, and see that what you see isn't always what you get. (Explanations on page 40.)

## A Friendly Ghost

In 1982, a family moved into an old house in Livermore, California. There was something warm and inviting about the house. After a few months, they began to feel that the house was haunted. Finally, 12-year-old Alan admitted that he had long conversations with the ghost. Her name was Lois. She was the previous owner of the house, who had died in 1980. She told Alan about her life, the house and the neighborhood—details that reportedly were later checked out and found to be true. She kept appearing in the house because she loved it. Besides, she really liked the new family and enjoyed watching TV with Alan.

Do you see birds or animals here?

Are the lines making up the square straight or curved?

# Boo!
## BOARD GAME

CROSSROADS
CROSSROADS

It's October 31—the spookiest night of the year. And where's the spookiest place to be? Many say that ghosts can be seen at crossroads on Halloween. So be very wary of the crossroad in this game. Any time you pass over the crossroads square, count it as a space. If you land on it, follow the instructions on the square.

Use only one die, and buttons or coins as counters. The player who rolls highest starts the game. Take turns rolling (only one roll allowed per turn) and moving counters. The winner is the first player to make it to the house that's been ghost-proofed with an unbroken circle on its door. You must roll the exact number to finish.

21

22

Friendly ghost helps you jump crossroad to square 24.

23

7   8

6, move this way

3 or 5, move this way

If you roll

2 or 4, move this way

Roman soldiers march straight through you. Run to crossroads!

6

1, move this way

9

24

5

10

25

Go straight to haunted house.

**Try to stay out of the Haunted House!**

Ghosts walk through doors, not you. Roll a 2 or 4 to proceed.

4

26

Ghost lights in cemetery light your way. Move ahead 4 spaces.

Miss a turn to cram ghost-busting salt in your pocket.

3

27

28

2

1

## START

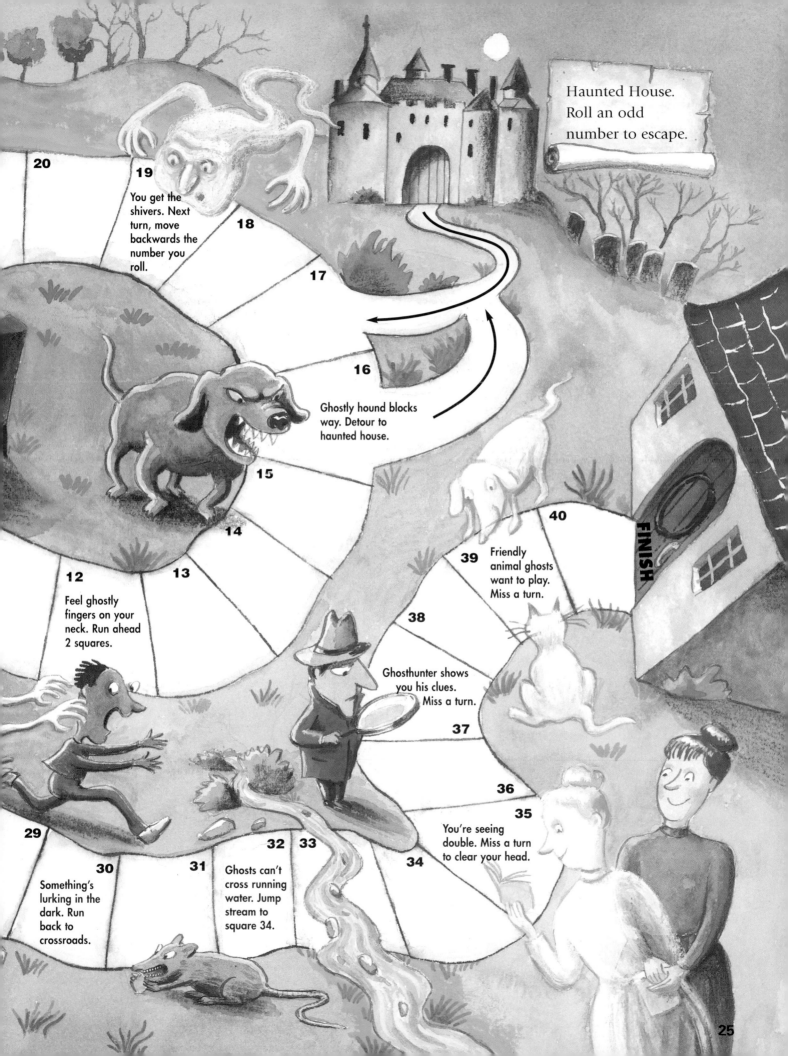

Haunted House. Roll an odd number to escape.

20

19 You get the shivers. Next turn, move backwards the number you roll.

18

17

16 Ghostly hound blocks way. Detour to haunted house.

15

14

13

12 Feel ghostly fingers on your neck. Run ahead 2 squares.

40

39 Friendly animal ghosts want to play. Miss a turn.

38 Ghosthunter shows you his clues. Miss a turn.

37

36

35 You're seeing double. Miss a turn to clear your head.

34

33

32 Ghosts can't cross running water. Jump stream to square 34.

31

30 Something's lurking in the dark. Run back to crossroads.

29

FINISH

25

## Living Ghosts

How would you feel if you walked into your kitchen and saw your brother raiding the fridge, then walked into the family room and saw the same brother watching TV? Unless you have identical twin brothers, you'd probably feel confused.

You would have just seen a doppelgänger (German for "double-goer"), a ghostly double of someone alive. A doppelgänger might be someone's energy body that has separated from its physical body and has become visible, an effect known as "astral traveling." Some people believe that astral traveling can happen while we sleep, like when you wake suddenly from a dream feeling as if you've just fallen back into your body.

Many ghostly encounters are said to be with the ghosts of living people. Emilie Sagée, a teacher in France in the late 19th century, is reported to have had a very active doppelgänger. It kept popping up all over the place, and eventually got her fired from her job. Imagine the panic in her classroom on the day when her students looked up from their workbooks to see two Mlle Sagées writing side by side on the chalkboard!

Some people even see their own doppelgängers. A Swiss student, working hard on a project, left his desk for a moment to get a reference book from the next room. As he was returning, he caught sight of himself still writing at the desk. He explained that he had the sensation of sitting and writing, and could even read what he was writing. Yet at the same time, he had the sensation of standing by the door, holding the cold metal doorknob. In amazement, he walked toward his sitting self—suddenly the double sensation ceased and he became one again.

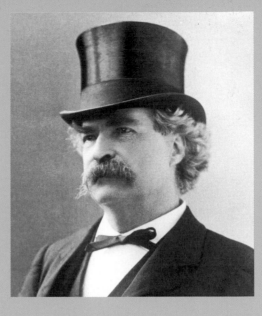

## Sorry, No Time to Change

The American writer Mark Twain (see above) once spotted a woman he knew at a large reception. Later that night he ran into her again at supper, wearing the same clothes she had on at the reception. So what's strange about that? At the time of the reception she had been on a train on her way into town. Could her ghostly double have been some kind of thought projection, sent out by her as she looked forward to the evening? In Norway, someone's double that arrives before they do is known as a vardøger.

## Double-Brainer

There might be medical explanations for seeing ghostly doubles. Seeing doppelgängers might originate from irritation in the region of the brain where the occipital, temporal and parietal lobes converge. Also, people who suffer from epilepsy or migraine headaches sometimes hallucinate and see lifelike images of themselves—doctors call it autoscopy.

parietal lobe

occipital lobe

temporal lobe

# Ghosts Attached to PEOPLE

If you have an OBE, or out-of-body-experience, you actually see yourself leaving your whole body below you.

## OBEs

Some believe that doppelgängers might be the result of an out-of-body-experience, OBE for short. The "near death experience" on page 9 is a type of OBE. During an OBE, you feel as though you're floating out of your body. You can pass through walls, and be anywhere instantly just by thinking about it. What if someone saw your energy body? Could you be mistaken for a ghost?

One psychologist, who experienced an OBE and investigated hundreds more, believes that everything that happens during an OBE happens inside the brain. Her explanation is that your brain uses information from your senses to build an idea of how you relate to the world around you. (If it didn't, you'd have to constantly remind yourself of things like which way was up.) Many OBEs occur in the dozy state just before falling asleep. If you slip into this half-aware "twilight zone" and your brain stops receiving information on what position your body is in, it will quickly make sense of what's happening by creating a new reality. But if you ever experience an OBE, don't worry that you're going crazy. Surveys show that normal, healthy people seem to have the most OBEs.

## Awake or Dreaming?

There's an old belief that if you fall in a dream and hit bottom, you'll die—it's not true. But there's a form of dreaming, called lucid dreaming, that might account for OBEs. In this unusual state, you're asleep and dreaming, but you know that you're dreaming. The trick to lucid dreaming is to keep doing a quick reality check. Ask yourself, "Am I awake or dreaming?" even when you think you're wide awake; look around you and think about what's happening. If some things seem a little odd, chances are you're dreaming. It takes a lot of practice to become a lucid dreamer, but once you get the hang of it, you can travel instantly to anywhere in the world you want to be, passing straight through walls just like a ghost.

## Hello Down There!

Why does the spooky experience of an OBE include the feeling of looking down on the world? With little information coming in from its senses, the brain relies on memory. Think about your memories of an event or a place—do you "see" it from a bird's-eye point of view? Most people do.

## Astral Homework

To find out whether OBEs involve astral traveling, a psychologist put 20 small objects into a box, and made lists of 20 common words and randomly selected five-digit numbers. Every Sunday night she picked one object out of the box; she wrote one of the numbers and one of the words from her lists on a sheet of paper and placed it next to the object in her kitchen. Her students had to try to identify what she'd written and the object she'd selected by astral traveling to her home during an OBE. During the lengthy time she ran the experiment, one person partially succeeded, but was unable to repeat it.

After Sir Ernest Shackleton's ship the *Endurance* was crushed in the ice floes around the Antarctic, Shackleton (inset) and a few of his best men set out on a grueling trip to get help—some of it ghostly.

## Strange Companions

**Mind if I come along on the trip?**

Explorer Sir Ernest Shackleton set sail in 1914, determined to be the first to lead an expedition across the Antarctic on foot. But the loss of his ship stranded the company more than a year later on Elephant Island. Shackleton led a few of his sailors across stormy oceans and an icy land route to a whaling station on South Georgia Island. As leader of a three-man rescue team back across a mountainous region of Antarctica in 1916, he wrote, "It often seemed to me that we were four, not three."

Shackleton isn't the only person to report spectral companions at times of grave danger. A pioneer American aviator, Edith Foltz-Stearns, once said that at times of great danger she didn't feel as if she were flying solo. A ghostly presence in the cockpit helped guide her to safety. She claimed that in 1932 the voice of a dead schoolmate warned her against making a risky landing, and she later credited her dead father with preventing her from crashing into a mountainside during a Second World War flying mission.

What these death-defying adventurers have in common, of course, is stress. They felt ghostly presences when they were struggling, both physically and mentally, to survive. Many mountaineers see ghosts at high altitude when they're climbing without the aid of oxygen. It seems that extreme stress and the lack of oxygen can have similar astonishing affects on the brain.

## How's Your Imagination?

Surveys show that creative people with active imaginations more frequently report sensations of floating or leaving their body, and the conviction that a strange being is standing to one side of them. Researchers have discovered creative people with active imaginations often have unusual bursts of electrical activity in the temporal lobes of their brain (just above the ears). This unusual electrical activity in the brain can also be caused by a lack of oxygen. Are OBEs and mysterious ghostly presences reported by mountaineers and explorers all connected to sudden, unusual surges of electricity in the brain?

## The Gray Man of Ben Macdhui

Mountaineers and explorers frequently describe the sensation of being accompanied by mysterious companions, and report seeing the ghosts of dead friends. Many climbers who have reached the summit of the Scottish mountain Ben Macdhui (see left) have reported sensing a mysterious presence. First a mist appears, then the climbers are filled with a sense of dread and a feeling that they're not alone. Unnerved, they set off down the mountain, only to hear footsteps following behind. Some climbers have even broken into a run and, to their horror, heard the footsteps speed up to keep up with them!

# Ghosts Attached to PEOPLE

This photograph shows a faint image of a man, supposedly Lord Combermere, sitting in his favorite chair while his funeral was taking place.

## Crisis Apparitions

A crisis apparition is the ghost of someone appearing at the moment of death—give or take a few hours. It usually appears once, presumably to warn people or maybe just to make contact one last time with a loved one, and is never seen again. This is one of the most frequently reported ghosts, and never more so than during times of war.

One evening in January, 1970, a young American woman settled down with some friends to watch President Nixon give his annual State of the Union Address. In the middle of the speech, she saw the picture change from the President to a jungle scene. Suddenly, to her horror, she realized she was looking at her fiancé, lying dead on the ground. None of her friends saw what she did on the TV screen, and they were amazed when she burst into tears and explained what she had seen. A week later, she received news that her fiancé had been killed in action in Vietnam on the night she saw him on TV.

Crisis apparitions aren't always of people who have just died. They can sometimes be of people who are going through a

## Coming Home

Many relatives and friends of people serving in the armed forces during the two World Wars had tales to tell of crisis apparitions. Perhaps they'd look up from what they were doing and through the window they'd see someone who'd been overseas walking up the path toward the door. Elated, they'd rush to fling open the door, only to discover there was no one there. Later, the news would arrive that the person had died at the time they were seen walking up the path.

## Sherbrooke's Sighting

Long before he became Governor-General of Canada in 1816, Sir John Sherbrooke was an army officer based in Sydney, Nova Scotia. He was visiting a fellow officer by the name of Wynyard, when they were both surprised to see a tall, pale young man appear in the doorway then walk through into the bedroom. It was Wynyard's brother, John. Both officers followed him into the bedroom but he'd disappeared. When news finally arrived from England they learned that John Wynyard had died there on the day they'd seen him in Nova Scotia.

### TEST YOUR TELEPATHIC POWERS

**1** Draw four simple pictures and place them in four identical envelopes.

**2** Invite a friend over and ask him or her to sit in another room with a pencil and paper.

**3** Shuffle the envelopes, open one and concentrate on its picture for five minutes.

**4** While you're concentrating, your friend draws whatever comes to mind.

**5** Open all the envelopes and ask your friend to select the picture that most resembles what he or she drew (it needn't be exact). Then reveal which one you were trying to send by telepathy.

**6** Repeat these five steps as many times as you can, recording each result. (Explanation page 40.)

terrible crisis, but survive it. So they can be living ghosts too. This twist suggests that crisis apparitions might be caused by telepathy, the direct communication of thoughts from one mind to another. But does telepathy really exist? Or are these fleeting glimpses of loved ones the result of wishful thinking on the part of people who are anxious for news of them?

## Ghosts with Attitude

Is your place haunted by an invisible spirit that throws things, makes terrible smells, spins lightbulbs in their sockets, repeatedly dials the same telephone numbers, breaks ornaments and slams doors and windows? Sounds like you've got a poltergeist (from the German *poltern*, meaning "to knock" and *geist*, meaning "spirit"). If you believe the movie of the same name, the first thing to do is check if your home is built over an ancient graveyard.

Experts on ghosts don't believe that poltergeists are ghosts, anyway. Why? A family thought that they had the typical poltergeist: the TV kept switching itself on and off, and the clock jumped across the mantelpiece. What experts found was that the

**Watch out for flying furniture!**

rattle of the dog's collar was the same frequency as the remote control unit: every time the dog scratched its neck in front of the TV, the set switched on or off. And the clock? It was so dirty inside that its main spring kept jamming, only to suddenly jerk free with such force that it propelled the clock forward. A leather collar for the dog and a good clock cleaning sent this poltergeist on its way!

Most poltergeist activity has a perfectly natural explanation (like dog collars and dirty clocks). Examples that aren't so easily explained tend to focus on a kid (usually a teenager) with emotional problems. Maybe a troubled teenager unknowingly creates the poltergeist as a way of letting off steam, subconsciously using mind power to make things move without touching them. Or maybe, as Harry Potter finds at Hogwarts school, mischievous ghosts just like hanging around kids!

## The Ghosts of Islington Green

During a family visit to London, England, our eight-year-old daughter slept in a room with a large oil painting over the mantel. Next morning I found the painting jammed behind a heavy oak chest across the room. Our host hadn't touched the painting and our daughter wasn't big enough to move it on her own. How, then, had it moved? Was someone playing a prank? Several years later a possible ghostly explanation was revealed. A developer was refused permission to excavate the area surrounding the house—the site of a medieval mass grave for victims of the plague.

## Judge Rules Poltergeists Exist!

A couple in Manhattan paid a deposit on a house only to discover that the seller had failed to mention it had a poltergeist. When the seller refused to give the couple their money back, the matter went before several courts of law. The final ruling was that the seller should have revealed the existence of the poltergeist and the would-be buyers had a right to a refund.

# Ghost-HUNTING

**Yikes!
I better hide.**

## Call the Ghosthunters

There really are ghosthunters. You might be disappointed to learn that their investigations usually turn up natural explanations for ghostly encounters. You've come across several explanations already, many of them having to do with the way your brain operates. Some unnerving experiences, such as strange noises in the dead of night or sudden bursts of cold air, can have far from supernatural causes. What might these be and how do ghosthunters find them?

The first thing a ghosthunter does, when asked to investigate spooky noises in a house, is research its history and find out whether there are any disused sewers, water channels or even ruins underneath it. If a house sits on ground in which water can rise and fall, the foundation of the house will also move. Each time the house settles, it can make some very weird noises. A sagging roof, cracks in the walls and doors that no longer shut properly all point to house movement, not ghosts, as the source of the noise.

Inside the house, a ghosthunter will check the plumbing and listen for rats and mice in the walls. In the dead of night, knocking noises from pipes can be scary and mice can sound as big as bears. And the tunnels that rodents make through the walls can be responsible for mysterious bursts of cold air. Sometimes small holes in the walls of a house that rises and sinks aren't visible all the time. A hole that's invisible when the house sinks will open up and allow cold air to seep through when the house rises again. It can also let in light, which might create the occasional ghostly image in a dusty room.

## Are You a Natural Ghosthunter?

You probably are if you can figure out how you'd use the following:

White sugar or flour
Black thread
A stethoscope
A stick of chalk

(Answer page 40)

## England's Most Haunted House?

Strange lights in locked rooms, slow dragging footsteps, a coach and horses galloping across the lawn and then vanishing, the sounds of the organ being played and bells ringing in the empty church, stones being thrown by an unseen hand, mysterious writing appearing on walls, the spectre of a nun walking the grounds in broad daylight—Borley Rectory (see below) seemed to be teeming with ghosts. It had a long history of ghost sightings, but the haunting activity went through the roof in the 1920s when a ghosthunter named Harry Price began investigating there. Price was accused of fraud, but Borley Rectory made his career as a ghosthunter before it burned down in 1939.

# HUNTING

Dr. Richard Wiseman of the University of Hertfordshire led one of the largest ghost hunts in recent times, in June 2000 in Hampton Court Palace in London, England. Did his thermal imaging camera capture evidence of a ghost like the one seen behind him? No, it was just a cleaner in period costume doing some early morning vacuuming.

## The Ultimate Ghost Hunt

Imagine a ghost hunt in an old haunted palace in England. You might picture people creeping through dusty corridors and secret passages, holding flashlights and waiting for the wailing to begin. In fact, the ghosthunt at Hampton Court Palace was well-organized and scientific. Each of 1000 volunteers was equipped with a floor plan and a questionnaire, and sent out to patrol a designated area of the palace for 20 minutes. They were to mark on the floor plan exactly where they experienced odd sensations and describe them on the questionnaire.

Every day, a scientific team from the University of Hertfordshire collected the information and analyzed it. Many people reported strange experiences: they felt dizzy or sick, or sensed some kind of presence. Slowly a pattern began to emerge: about half of the experiences took place at a few precise locations.

## The Haunted Gallery

Henry VIII's fifth wife, Catherine Howard, was charged with being unfaithful to her husband and sentenced to death. When she was first accused, she ran into the chapel at Hampton Court Palace (see below) to plead for her life. Henry ignored her and she was dragged, screaming, the full length of the gallery. Catherine was beheaded, but people say her ghost is still seen and heard as it screams its way along the Hampton Court Gallery more than 450 years later.

Every night the ghosthunting team set up their instruments: a video camera, a magnetometer to measure electromagnetic activity, temperature sensors and a thermal imaging camera that detects heat energy in the dark. They watched their instrument readings carefully for any sudden bursts of activity coinciding with an image appearing on the video. Alas, they didn't find any. But they located several drafts, which could account for sudden temperature drops.

Will ghosthunters like these eventually find logical explanations for ghosts? For now, tricks of the mind, jangling dog collars, telepathy, quantum mechanics, subsiding houses, tunneling mice, recordings in stone, disappearing holes and all the other possible explanations can't account for all supernatural encounters. And it wouldn't be much fun if they did! Whether ghosts do or do not exist outside of our minds, our imaginations are richer for them, and we'll insist that they stick around for a long time to come.

Boohoo—
that's the end.

## ANSWERS

Are You Superstitious?, page 13

1 Salt used to be such a precious substance that spilling it was bad luck. Spilled salt thrown over the left side of the body is supposed to hit evil spirits lurking there in the eye!

2 A poem is probably the source of the superstitious fear of stepping on sidewalk cracks:
*Step in a hole, and you'll break your mother's bowl / Step on a crack, and you'll break your mother's back / Step in a ditch, and your mother's nose will itch / Step on the dirt, and you'll tear your father's shirt / etc.*

3 There was a type of hanging gallows that was propped against a supporting beam, like a ladder leaning against a building. This might be the source of the superstition against walking under ladders.

Don't Believe Your Eyes, page 23

• Your brain loves to pick out patterns. You can stare at this image and see a group of birds with open beaks. Then, your brain registers another pattern, and the birds turn into rabbits.

• Put a pencil or a rule along the lines that make up the square, and you'll see they are straight. The curved lines behind the figure fool you into seeing the square as curvy.

Test Your Telepathic Powers, page 33

Work out the average result by comparing successful selections with number of tries. If only chance is at work, the test should give the correct result once in every four tests. If you get more or less than this, something other than chance might be at work!

Are You a Natural Ghosthunter?, page 37

Here's how a ghosthunter uses the following items:

• White sugar or flour sprinkled on the floor lets you hear non-ghostly footsteps, or lets you see where someone has walked.

• Black thread strung between furniture and across hallways or doorways makes an invisible obstacle course for phony ghosts in the dark.

• A doctor's stethoscope is excellent for listening for mice and rats in the walls.

• A stick of chalk comes in handy to outline furniture on the floor or against walls, so you can easily see if it has been moved.